ZOOBILEE ZOO™
Best Friends

ZOOBILEE ZOO™
Best Friends

by Jan Carr
illustrated by Carol Hudson

SCHOLASTIC INC.

New York Toronto London Auckland Sydney

ISBN 0-590-41047-4

12 11 10 9 8 7 6 5 4 3 2 1   7 8 9/8 0 1 2/9

Printed in the U.S.A.   24

First Scholastic printing, September 1987

One bright morning, the Magical Mayor Ben was sitting on
his balcony and looking out over all of Zoobilee Zoo when
he heard singing:

> Best friends
> Till the end
> Together forever

"Mmm," he said. "Catchy little tune. That must be Whazzat."

And indeed it was. For just down the way, Whazzat Kangaroo was in her house, planning a surprise for her good friend, Talkatoo Cockatoo. Whazzat was composing a song at her piano: a special song that she was writing just for Talkatoo.

"I think I'll call it 'Fine Feathered Friend,'" Whazzat said.

Whazzat just loved music. "And I love my friend, Talkatoo," she said. "I really don't know which I love better. Hmmm. Both, I guess."

She finished the last lines and sang:

Best friends
Till the end
Together forever
Together we'll weather
Every bad storm
We'll keep each other warm
On a scary night
We'll hold each other tight
We'll share the good times, too
Together me and you
Till the very end
My fine feathered friend

Of course, Whazzat couldn't wait for Talkatoo to hear her song. "She's going to be so surprised. So, so, <u>sooooo</u> surprised!" said Whazzat.

She grabbed her kazoo and hurried out the door.

At first, no one answered at Talkatoo's. But when Whazzat knocked again, Talkatoo burst through the door.

"Oh, dear, it's you," said Talkatoo. "I thought it was Bravo. I'm lo sate! I mean, so late! Must hurry! Must hurry!"

And she ran right past Whazzat and down the lane.

"Talkatoo!" Whazzat ran after her. "Wait a minute! I want you to hear my new song."

Talkatoo kept running.

"Wait up!" shouted Whazzat. "I want you to hear my new song!"

Talkatoo ran on.

"Talkatoo!" Whazzat cried louder. "LISTEN TO MY SONG!"
Talkatoo stopped.
"Not now," she said. "I don't have time. Bravo is waiting
for me. We're going to write a play together."
And off she ran.

Whazzat sat down in front of Bill der Beaver's house. Her eyes welled up with tears.

Just then, Bill der Beaver walked by. When he saw Whazzat crying, he set his toolbox on the grass and sat down beside her.

"Why, Whazzat," he asked, "what's the matter?"

Whazzat told Bill the whole miserable story.

"Talkatoo doesn't want to be my friend anymore. She only wants to be with Bravo. She wouldn't even listen to my new song that I wrote especially for her."

Bill der Beaver was surprised. Whazzat and Talkatoo were such good friends—best friends.

"She must not have understood what you meant," he said. "She must not know that you wrote a special <u>friendship</u> song. You ought to go over to Bravo's theater and explain."

When Whazzat arrived, Bravo and Talkatoo were pacing back and forth onstage. Bravo was throwing his arms around and gesturing wildly.

"It needs something else," he said. "It needs something …more."

"More words," Talkatoo suggested. "I'll write more words."

"No, no, no," said Bravo. "It needs something…really… <u>grand!</u>"

Just then, Whazzat peeked around the curtain.
"Psst, Talkatoo," she said. "Can I talk to you a minute?"
"Not now," said Talkatoo. "I'm busy."
"But I have to tell you something important," said
Whazzat. "I have to explain something."

From center stage, Bravo Fox glared at Whazzat.

"My dear Kangaroo," he said, "can't you see that we are working? Talkatoo is helping me with something very important. We are writing a play."

"Oh," said Whazzat. Feeling very hurt, she ran off to find Bill der Beaver.

Bravo and Talkatoo didn't notice. They had already gone back to working on their play. They were still having the same problems as before. Talkatoo was coming up with lots of ideas, but Bravo didn't like any of them.

"The play needs something different, something that gives it more rhythm," said Bravo. "It needs, I don't know, a little trill."

They sat down on the stage, their heads in their hands. They couldn't think of any way at all to fix the play.

Whazzat found Bill der Beaver and told him what had happened. The more Whazzat talked, the angrier she got.

"Talkatoo thinks she's some kind of big shot," said Whazzat. "Boy, would I like to get even with her."

Bill der Beaver had an idea. He grabbed Whazzat's hand, and together they ran back to the theater.

When they got there, Whazzat and Bill sat down right next to the stage. Whazzat took out her kazoo. Bill opened up his toolbox and took out a hammer and a piece of tin.

"Ready?" he asked.

"Ready," said Whazzat.

Then the two of them began to play Whazzat's song— as loudly as they could.

<u>Best friends</u>
<u>Till the end</u>
<u>Together forever</u>
<u>Together we'll weather</u>
<u>Every bad storm</u>
<u>We'll keep each other warm</u>....

"Excuse me, Whazzat," said Talkatoo. "I can't hear myself think."

"Sorry. Can't talk. I'm busy," said Whazzat.

> On a scary night
> We'll hold each other tight....

"Whazzat!" Talkatoo said again. "Could you please stop that?"

"Very busy. Very important," said Whazzat.

> We'll share the good times, too
> Together me and you....

"STOP THAT NOISE!" shouted Talkatoo.

None of the Zoobles can quite remember exactly what it was that happened after that. But they do remember that Whazzat really lost her temper. "Talkatoo, you're just a big old feather duster!"

All this took Talkatoo completely by surprise. She didn't know why Whazzat was so upset.

"Of course Whazzat's upset!" Bill chimed in. "Whazzat wrote a song for you, and you don't even care!"

"Oh," Talkatoo said quietly. She just hadn't realized. Talkatoo felt very ashamed.

Meanwhile, Bravo Fox, who stood off to the side, didn't even hear the shouting. He was thinking of the song and was humming the melody in his head.

"Whazzat, my dear, what a charming little tune," he said.

Then he started pacing. "Why, that song is just what we've been looking for. It's perfect for the play," he said.

"It is?" Whazzat asked.

"In fact," said Bravo, "I think we need more music. Lots and lots of music.

"Eureka!" cried Bravo. "I've got it! We won't write just a play. We'll write a musical! And Whazzat can help!"

Whazzat looked at Talkatoo. She wasn't sure that she wanted to work on a musical. Not if Talkatoo would be working on it, too.

But Talkatoo looked right back at her and smiled. "Please?" asked Talkatoo. And she meant it.

All the rest of that week, the four Zoobles worked on
the project. Whazzat and Talkatoo worked together, writing
the music and the words. Bill der Beaver built the scenery.
And Bravo Fox kept busy telling everybody what to do.
He was the director.

On opening night, everyone was excited. All the other Zoobles had come to see the new musical, which Bravo Fox called <u>Best Friends</u>. The story was about two good friends who fight but then make up.

Whazzat sang the very last song:

<u>Though some days we may fight</u>
<u>It will all turn out all right</u>
<u>When we talk things through</u>
<u>Together me and you</u>
<u>Our differences will mend</u>
<u>My fine feathered friend</u>

Then the curtain came down, and all the Zoobles applauded. It was the best musical they had ever seen.

ZOOBILEE ZOO™

THINGS TO DO!

MAKE A KAZOO!

Whazzat Kangaroo has a kazoo.
Now you can have one, too.
Here's what you will need:
> a comb (use a new one and wash it first)
> a piece of wax paper
> tape

1. Fold the piece of wax paper in half.

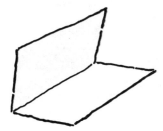

2. Put the comb inside the wax paper.

4. Your kazoo is ready to play. Place the comb between your lips and hum a tune!

3. Tape the two halves of wax paper around the comb.

TELL A STORY!

Make up a story to go with the pictures.

PICTURE THIS!

Draw a picture of your best friend.